The SHINY SKATES

Story and Pictures

by

Elizabeth Koda-Callan

WORKMAN PUBLISHING, NEW YORK

Library of Congress Cataloging-in-Publication Data

Koda-Callan, Elizabeth.
The shiny skates/written and illustrated by Elizabeth Koda-Callan.
p.   cm.

Summary: A young girl is discouraged when she has difficulty
learning to ice skate, until her mother gives her a special necklace.
Includes tiny silver skates on a silver chain tucked inside the cover.

ISBN 1-56305-309-8
[1. Ice skating—Fiction. 2. Self-confidence—Fiction.]
I. Title   92-50293
PZ7.K8175Sh 1992   CIP
[E]—dc20   AC

Workman books are available at special discounts
when purchased in bulk for premiums and sales promotions
as well as for fund-raising or educational use. Special editions
or book excerpts can also be created to specification.
For details, contact the Special Sales Director at the address below.

Workman Publishing Company
708 Broadway
New York, New York 10003
Printed in China
First printing October 1992
10 9 8 7 6 5 4 3

For Jane Rosenberg Porter
and
Jennifer, Chase and Lacey

Once there was a little girl who dreamed of being a skater. She pictured herself gliding across the ice even while her feet were firmly on the ground.

The little girl's parents knew of her dream and gave her a pair of white figure skates for her birthday. "Oh, what beautiful skates!" she said as she opened the present. "Now I can really learn to skate."

The next day the little girl and her friend went to test her new skates at a nearby rink. The little girl put them on and wobbled toward the skating area, but when she got on the ice she found that she could barely stand up. Her feet were slipping and sliding.

Her friend, who was already a good skater, tried to show her how to move forward. As the little girl put one foot in front of the other, her feet slipped out from under her and she tumbled backward on the ice. "Ouch!" she cried and her face became very red. "Ice skating isn't as easy as it looks," she said as her friend helped her up.

All afternoon the little girl struggled to keep her balance. She went home tired and discouraged.

A few days later, an invitation to her friend's skating party arrived in the mail. "I don't think I want to go to the party," the little girl told her mother.

"Why not?" asked her mother. "You can wear your new skates."

"I can't skate and everyone else will know how. I won't have a good time," the little girl answered.

"Ever since you've gotten your new skates, you've been thinking about taking skating lessons," said her mother. "The party is still several weeks away, so this might be the perfect time to start them."

Later that day, as the little girl was putting her figure skates away, her mother came into her room. She sat down in a chair beside the little girl. "You know, I remember feeling discouraged with my first try at skating, too," she said. "I found something special that helped me and that might help you."

The little girl's mother handed her an old yellowed envelope tied with a lavender ribbon. The little girl untied the ribbon and opened the envelope. There, inside, were two silver skates on a silver necklace. "Your grandmother gave me these skates as a gift when I was learning to skate," said her mother. "And now I'd like you to have them. They will remind you that you *can* skate, if you just do your best. Give yourself another chance."

The little girl admired the tiny shiny skates. They were so shiny that they almost seemed to glow with their own light. She imagined herself gliding across the ice, wearing shiny skates just like the skates on the necklace. The little girl gave her mother a big hug. "Thank you," she said. "I think I will take skating lessons after all." She put on the necklace and decided to wear it to her first class.

It took several lessons before the little girl felt comfortable on the ice. But she learned quickly.

First she learned to skate forward,
and then she practiced how to stop.

She soon learned to skate backward,
and after practicing steadily, she could

even do front crossovers. At every lesson
she wore the shiny skates.

The little girl improved, but she still felt that she wasn't good enough to go to the party.

The night before the party she received a phone call from her friend. "Are you coming to my party tomorrow?" her friend asked.

"I'm not sure. I'm not a very good skater," said the little girl.

"It doesn't matter," answered her friend. "It's just a party. You'll have fun. You don't have to be an Olympic champion."

"Thanks," answered the little girl. "I guess I'll come."

The day of the skating party arrived. The little girl was excited as she dressed in her favorite skating outfit. She put on a heavy green sweater, a pleated red skating skirt, red tights and a red headband. And around her neck she wore the shiny skates. But the closer the time came to leave for the party, the more nervous the little girl became. "What if everyone can skate better than I can? What if no one wants to skate with me? What if I fall and look silly?" she thought to herself.

The little girl glanced down and the glistening tiny skates caught her eye. She held them in her hand and remembered what her mother had said. "These shiny skates are special," she thought. "They remind me that I have practiced and learned to skate. I may not be perfect, but I will go and do my best."

Soon it was time to leave and the little girl's father drove her to the skating rink. She said goodbye to him and sat down on a bench where people were putting on their skates. Some of her friends were already there. After putting on her own skates, she walked gingerly over large rubber mats toward the ice.

It was then she noticed something she didn't expect.

As she stood at the edge of the rink, she saw that not everyone was skating well. Some children couldn't even skate at all, though they were having fun trying. She was surprised that things could be so different from what she had imagined. She wondered why she had been worried in the first place.

While the little girl stood and watched, her friend skated up to her. "Hi! I'm glad you came," she said. "Let's skate."

The little girl got on the ice with her friend and they began to skate together. They went around the rink several times, and the little girl didn't wobble or fall. "Wow!" her friend said. "You're a good skater now. You must have practiced a lot."

The little girl smiled to herself. She was pleased that she had practiced so hard.

Later that afternoon, the little girl saw someone who was struggling alone at the edge of the rink. She skated up to her. "I know learning to skate isn't easy," she said as she took her hand. "Just do your best." The little girl helped her new friend skate that afternoon. They skated and fell and laughed together. They had a wonderful time.

The little girl was happy that she had decided to go to the party after all. For it was there that the little girl, wearing the shiny skates, glided across the ice — just as she had always dreamed she would.

And so, she discovered that doing her best was very good indeed.

About the Author

Elizabeth Koda-Callan is a designer, illustrator and best-selling children's book author who lives in New York City. Her favorite place to skate as a young girl was a small, wooded pond in Connecticut, where she grew up.

She is the creator of the Magic Charm book series, which includes THE MAGIC LOCKET, THE SILVER SLIPPERS, THE GOOD LUCK PONY, and THE TINY ANGEL.